A Home in the Snow

Written by Peter Bently

Illustrated by Charles Fuge

Bramble was off to fetch wood with his sleigh.
He smiled to himself, "It's my birthday today!

A
Home
in the
Snow

First published in Great Britain in 2019 by Hodder and Stoughton

Text copyright © Peter Bently, 2019
Illustrations copyright © Charles Fuge, 2019

A CIP catalogue record of this book
is available from the British Library.

HB ISBN: 978 1 444 94036 7
PB ISBN: 978 1 444 94037 4

10 9 8 7 6 5 4 3 2 1

Printed and bound in China.

Hodder Children's Books
An imprint of
Hachette Children's Group
Part of Hodder and Stoughton
Carmelite House
50 Victoria Embankment
London EC4Y 0DZ

An Hachette UK Company
www.hachette.co.uk

www.hachettechildrens.co.uk

Hodder
Children's
Books

I'll make my home cosy and warm as can be
in case any friends want to come round for tea."

He saw his pal Pippin, who hurried away.
"I've left something baking," she called. "I can't stay!"
Bramble waved back as the stoat scurried by.
She's forgotten my birthday, he thought with a sigh.

Soon afterwards, Bramble saw Tipper the Toad,
who said, "Can you give me a lift with my load?
I'm going to Pippin's for afternoon tea
and I promised to bring her some firewood, you see."

They hadn't gone far when Bramble saw Boo,
who was trudging along towards Pippin's house too.
"She's asked me to tea. It sounds rather jolly.
I said that I'd bring her a few sprigs of holly."

The sleigh was becoming a little bit full
and Bramble was finding it heavy to pull.
But he didn't mind helping out Tipper and Boo –
though neither had said, "Happy Birthday to You."

Snuffle was gathering nuts by a tree.

She said, "They're for Pippin. I'm off there for tea."

Bramble smiled kindly. "It sounds like great fun.

Perhaps you could bring me a leftover bun."

Bramble tramped steadily on through the snow.
He thought to himself, "Well, it's not far to go.
I love all my friends and I do hate to moan
but it looks like I'm spending my birthday alone."

"I'll drop them at Pippin's
then make my own tea.
I'll just have to sing
Happy Birthday to Me."

The path down to Pippin's house came into view.

"Wait, there's a quicker way, Bramble!" said Boo.

"Good idea," agreed Snuffle. "Let's go straight ahead!"

"Through the woods?" wondered Bramble.

"Oh yes!" Tipper said.

On Bramble went through the silvery trees.
The snow was so deep, it came over his knees.

His breath turned to mist in the icy cold chill
and the wintery woodland was silent and still.

Sunbeams shone brightly on patches of white.
Icicles glistened like crystals of light.

Bramble stomped on as the sky turned to red.

"We're right in the middle of nowhere!" he said.

"Don't worry," grinned Snuffle. "It's not very far.

When we get through those bushes, you'll see where we are."

It was tricky to push all the branches aside.

What Bramble saw next made his eyes open wide . . .

"Welcome, dear Bramble!" said Pippin with glee.

"I hope you enjoy your SURPRISE BIRTHDAY TEA!"

"It was so hard to keep it a secret," said Boo.

"But we managed," laughed Tipper. "The others did too!"

"The others?" said Bramble. And then, all around . . .

. . . from out of the wood came a murmuring sound.
And in the dark shadows moved bright spots of light,
growing bigger and bigger as they came into sight.

Then dozens of animals stepped from the wood
and sang "HAPPY BIRTHDAY!" as loud as they could.

"Good gracious!" gasped Bramble. "What a lovely surprise!
Excuse me ... I seem to have smoke in my eyes."

After the tea,
they danced in the snow,
then they all snuggled up
in the bonfire's warm glow.

They sat round the fire and thrilled with delight
as Bramble told tales in the deepening night.

"Thanks for my lovely surprise," Bramble said
as he gazed at the stars shining bright overhead.
"I thought I'd be spending my birthday alone,
but I wouldn't have had any fun on my own."

He turned to his friends, and chuckled to see
they were all sleeping soundly, as snug as can be.
"Your home's where your heart is, that's one thing I know.
So my home is here, with dear friends in the snow."

For my family - P.B.

For Zephanie, who has a home by a stream - C.F.